THIS BOOK

BELONGS TO:

THE STORY OF *Miss Moppet*

THE STORY OF
MISS MOPPET

BY

BEATRIX POTTER

FREDERICK WARNE

FREDERICK WARNE

Published by the Penguin Group
Penguin Books Ltd, 80 Strand, London WC2R ORL, England
Penguin Young Readers Group, 345 Hudson Street, New York, New York 10014, USA
Penguin Group (Canada), 90 Eglinton Avenue East, Suite 700, Toronto,
Ontario, Canada M4P 2Y3
Penguin Ireland, 25 St Stephen's Green, Dublin 2, Ireland
Penguin (Group) Australia, 250 Camberwell Road, Camberwell, Victoria 3124, Australia
Penguin Books India (P) Ltd, 11 Community Centre,
Panchsheel Park, New Delhi 110 017, India
Penguin Books (NZ) Ltd, Cnr Rosedale and Airborne Roads,
Albany, Auckland 1310, New Zealand
Penguin Books (South Africa) (Pty) Ltd, PO Box 9, Parklands 2121, South Africa

Penguin Books Ltd, Registered Offices: 80 Strand, London WC2R ORL, England

Web site at: www.peterrabbit.com

First published by Frederick Warne 1906
This edition with reset text and new reproductions of Beatrix Potter's
illustrations first published 2002

Colour reproduction by
EAE Creative Colour Ltd, Norwich
Printed and bound in China

0707

THIS IS A PUSSY called Miss Moppet, she thinks she has heard a mouse!

This is the Mouse peeping out behind the cupboard, and making fun of Miss Moppet. He is not afraid of a kitten.

THIS is Miss Moppet jumping just too late; she misses the Mouse and hits her own head.

SHE thinks it is a very hard cupboard!

THE Mouse watches Miss Moppet from the top of the cupboard.

Miss Moppet ties up her head in a duster, and sits before the fire.

The Mouse thinks she is looking very ill. He comes sliding down the bell-pull.

Miss Moppet looks worse and worse. The Mouse comes a little nearer.

Miss Moppet holds her poor head in her paws, and looks at him through a hole in the duster. The Mouse comes *very* close.

AND then all of a sudden – Miss Moppet jumps upon the Mouse!

AND because the Mouse has teased Miss Moppet – Miss Moppet thinks she will tease the Mouse; which is not at all nice of Miss Moppet.

SHE ties him up in the duster,
and tosses it about like a ball.

BUT she forgot about that hole in the duster; and when she untied it – there was no Mouse!

He has wriggled out and run away; and he is dancing a jig on the top of the cupboard!

The End